P9-BZD-455

Roger and Matthew

By
Michel Thériault

Illustrations by
Magali Ben

English translation by
Pamela Doll

Fitzhenry & Whiteside

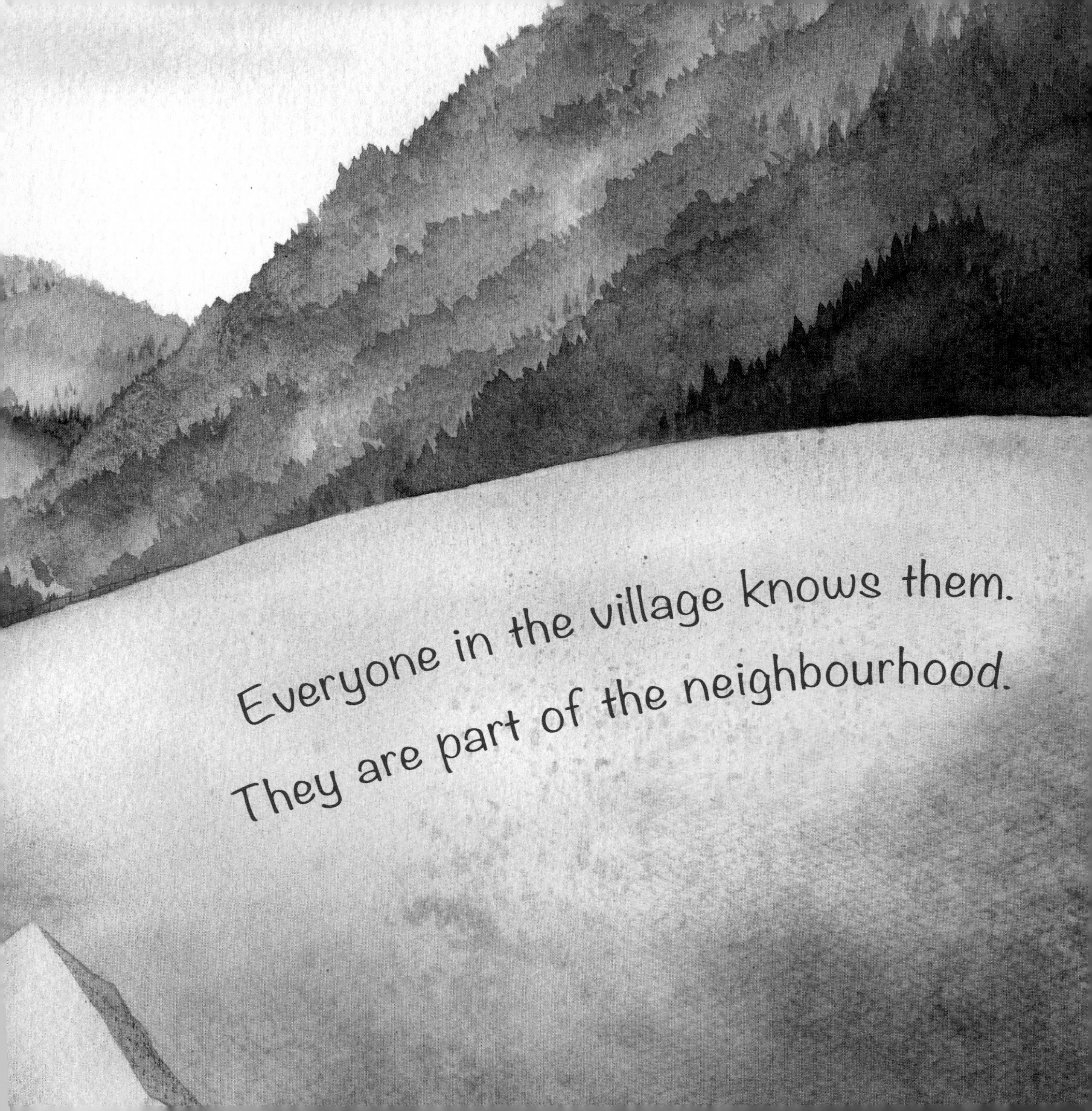

Everyone in the village knows them.
They are part of the neighbourhood.

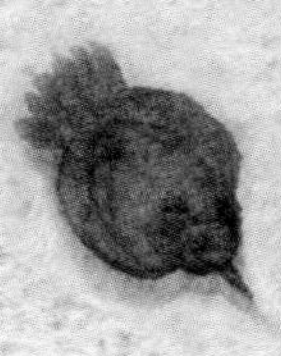

They are two old gentlemen.
One was an English teacher
and the other was a shopkeeper.

They are retired now.

CAHIER

They have been friends
since grade school.

They don't need words
to understand each other.

In their home there is sunlight.

There are flowers and sleepy cats.

Roger and Matthew
are two kind gentlemen.

Because they were different
people were often mean to them

and sometimes hurt them.

They weathered these storms
with pride and with courage.
They did not falter.

Their hearts are full
of happiness and truth.

In their home
there is love.
There are flowers and
birds singing in the backyard.

Roger and Matthew
are two kind gentlemen...

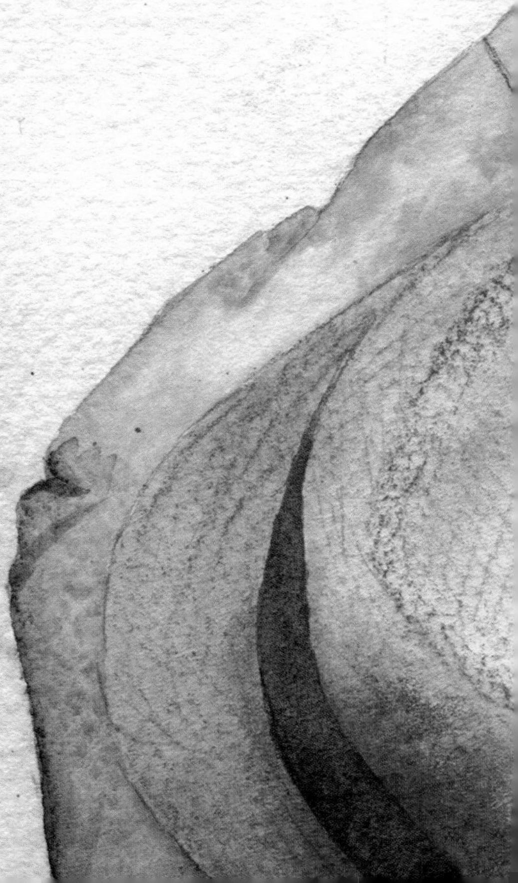

Roger and Matthew are in love.

Published in Canada by Fitzhenry & Whiteside
195 Allstate Parkway, Markham, ON L3R 4T8

Published in the United States by Fitzhenry & Whiteside
311 Washington Street, Brighton, MA 02135

Originally published as Ils sont…by Bouton d'or Acadie inc

2 4 6 8 10 7 5 3 1

Fitzhenry & Whiteside acknowledges with thanks the Canada Council for the Arts and the Ontario Arts Council for their support of our publishing program. We acknowledge the financial support of the Government of Canada through the Canada Book Fund (CBF) for our publishing activities.

Library and Archives Canada Cataloguing in Publication
Title: Roger and Matthew / by Michel Thériault ; illustrations by Magali Ben.
Other titles: Ils sont. English
Names: Thériault, Michel, 1957- author. | Ben, Magali, illustrator.
Description: Translation of: Ils sont.
Identifiers: Canadiana 20200181998 | ISBN 9781554554843 (hardcover)
Subjects: LCGFT: Picture books.
Classification: LCC PS8639.H473 I4713 2020 | DDC jC813/.6—dc23

Publisher Cataloging-in-Publication Data (U.S.)
Names: Thériault, Michel, 1957- , author. | Ben, Magali, illustrator.
Title: Roger and Matthew / by Michel Thériault ; illustrations by Magali Ben.
Description: Markham, Ontario : Fitzhenry & Whiteside, 2020. | Originally published in French as Ils sont. | Summary: "Same-sex couples were not always well accepted in society, but love and beauty always triumph! Two boys are friends, two boys are aging together, two old men are… in love! The singer-songwriter Michel Thériault attaches a new string to his bow and the illustrator Magali Ben seduces with his exceptional colors!" —Provided by publisher.
Identifiers: ISBN 978-1-55455-484-3 (hardcover)
Subjects: LCSH: Gay couples—Juvenile fiction. | Friendship – Juvenile friendship. | BISAC: JUVENILE FICTION / LGBT. | JUVENILE FICTION / Social Themes / Friendship.
Classification: LCC PZ7.T447Ro |DDC [F] – dc23

English translation by Pamela Doll.
Printed in Hong Kong by Sheck Wah Tong Printing

Fitzhenry & Whiteside